Louise Chandler Moulton

Swallow-Flights

Louise Chandler Moulton

Swallow-Flights

ISBN/EAN: 9783337015794

Printed in Europe, USA, Canada, Australia, Japan

Cover: Foto ©Andreas Hilbeck / pixelio.**de**

More available books at **www.hansebooks.com**

SWALLOW-FLIGHTS.

BY

LOUISE CHANDLER MOULTON.

London:

MACMILLAN AND CO.

1878.

[All Rights reserved.]

Dear eyes that read these lines of mine
  As you have read my heart ;
Forgive, since you the one divine,
  The other's lack of art.

CONTENTS.

CONTENTS.

CONTENTS.

SWALLOW-FLIGHTS.

FORTH from the wind-swept Country of my Heart
               Fly fast, swift wings !
For hence the summers and their suns depart—
               Here no bird sings.

With spring that country was all verdurous
               When first you came—
Its leafage with sweet songs solicitous,
               Its skies aflame

With dreaming of the summer's warm delights ;
               .Streams sought the sea :
White moons made beautiful the waiting nights :
               Your wings were free—

B

But here you nested through the smiling spring,
     Through summer too—
'Tis autumn now, and pleasant things take wing,
     So why not you?

Fly hence, and carry with you all my dreams,
     My hopes, my fears—
Shall I while sitting by Life's frozen streams,
     Weep idle tears?

Fly hence, swift wings—I have been glad with you
     In Life's glad spring,
Heard summer songs and thought their promise true :
     But now—take wing.

You are not doves that you should bring back leaves,
     From whelming seas—
Fly far, swift truants, from my silent eaves ;
     Leave me but peace.

November, 1877.

SWALLOW-FLIGHTS.

MAY-FLOWERS.

IF you catch a breath of sweetness,
　　And follow the odorous hint
Through woods where the dead leaves rustle,
　　And the golden mosses glint,

Along the spicy sea-coast,
　　Over the desolate down,
You will find the dainty May-flowers
　　When you come to Plymouth town.

Where the shy Spring tends her darlings,
　　And hides them away from sight,
Pull off the covering leaf-sprays,
　　And gather them pink and white—

Tinted by mystical moonlight,
  Freshened by frosty dew,
Till the fair, transparent blossoms
  To their pure perfection grew—

Then carry them home to your Lady,
  For flower of the spring is she—
Pink and white, and dainty and slight,
  And lovely as Love can be.

Shall they die because of her beauty ?
  Shall they live because she is sweet?
They will know the fate they were born for,
  But you—must wait at her feet.

MY SUMMER.

Do you think the summer will ever come,
   With white of lily and flush of rose—
With the warm, bright days of joy and June,
   So long you dream they will never close?

Will the birds, atilt on the bending boughs,
   Sing out their hearts in a mad delight;
And the golden butterflies, sun-suffused,
   Shimmer and shine from morn till night?

Do you think *my* summer will ever come,
   With brow of lily and cheek of rose?
Shall I hold her fast—my joy, my June—
   And dream that my day will never close?

Will she mock the birds on the bending boughs,
   (For her voice is music—my heart's delight!)
Or be content, like the butterflies,
   In the sun of my love from morn till night?

MORNING GLORY.

EARTH'S awake 'neath the laughing skies,
    After the dewy and dreamy night—
Riot of roses and Babel of birds,
    All the world in a whirl of delight.

Roses smile in their white content,
    Roses blush in their crimson bliss,
As the vagrant breezes, wooing them,
    Ruffle their petals with careless kiss.

Yellow butterflies flutter and float,
    Jewelled humming-birds glitter and glow,
And scorning the ways of such idle things
    Bees flit busily to and fro.

The mocking-bird swells his anxious throat,
    Trying to be ten birds in one ;
And the swallow twitters and dives and darts
    Into the azure to find the sun.

But robin red-breast builds his house,
    Singing a song of the joy to come,
And the oriole trims his golden vest,
    Glad to be back in his last year's home.

Lilies that sway on their slender stalks,
    Morning-glories that nod to the breeze,
Bloom of blossoms, and joy of birds—
    What in the world is better than these?

A PAINTED FAN.

Roses and butterflies snared on a fan,
   All that is left of a summer gone by ;
Of swift, bright wings that flashed in the sun,
   And loveliest blossoms that bloomed to die ;

By what subtle spell did you lure them here—
   Fixing a beauty that will not change—
Roses whose petals never will fall,
   Bright, swift wings that never will range ?

Had you owned but the skill to snare as well
   The swift-winged hours that came and went,
To prison the words that in music died,
   And fix with a spell the heart's content,

Then had you been of magicians the chief ;
　And loved and lovers should bless your art,
If you could but have painted the soul of the thing,
　Not the rose alone, but the rose's heart !

Flown are those days with their winged delights,
　As the odour is gone from the summer rose ;
Yet still, whenever I wave my fan,
　The soft, south wind of memory blows.

"AUTOMNE."

(FROM HAMON'S PICTURE.)

O, glad and free was Love until the fall ;
  Then came a spirit on the frosty air
To chill with icy breath the summer's bloom,
  And Love lies with the blossoms blighted there.

He throve so kindly all the summer time—
  Not warmer was the rose's crimson heart ;
Dews fell to bless him, and the soft winds blew,
  And gentle rains shed tears to ease his smart.

Through long June days and burning August noons
  The flowers and Love stole sweetness from the
    sun ;
Then summer went—the days grew brief and cold,
  The short, sweet lives of summer things were
    done.

No butterfly flits through November's gloom,
  No bird-note quivers on its frosty air :
Sweet Love had wings, and would have flown away,
  But Autumn chilled him with the blossoms there.

OUT IN THE SNOW.

Snow and silence came down together,
  Through the night so white and so still,
And young folks, housed from the bitter weather—
  Housed from the storm and the chill—

Heard in their dreams the sleigh-bells jingle,
  Coasted the hillsides under the moon,
Felt their cheeks with the keen air tingle,
  Skimmed the ice with their steel-clad shoon.

They saw the snow when they rose in the morning,
  Glittering ghost of the vanished night,
Though the sun shone clear in the winter dawning,
  And the day with a frosty pomp was bright.

Out in the clear cold winter weather—
  Out in the winter air like wine—
Kate with her dancing scarlet feather,
  Bess with her peacock plumage fine,

Joe and Jack with their pealing laughter,
  Frank and Tom with their gay hallo,
And half a score of roisterers after,
  Out in the witching, wonderful snow !

Shivering gray-beards shuffle and stumble,
  Righting themselves with a frozen frown,
Grumbling at every snowy tumble—
  But young folks know why the snow came down !

A QUEST.

ALL in the summer even,
  When sea and sky were bright,
As royally the sunset
  Went forth to meet the night,

My Love and I were sailing
  Into the shining West,
To find some Happy Island,
  Some Paradise of rest.

We steered where sunset splendour
  Made golden all the shore—
The rocks behind its brightness
  Were cruel as before.

Within the caves sang sirens,
    But there the whirlpools be ;
Not there the happy islands,
    Not there the peaceful sea.

Toward the deep mid-ocean
    Tides ran and swift winds blew ;
It must be there those islands
    Await the longing view.

Their shores are soft with verdure,
    Their skies for ever fair,
And always is the fragrance
    Of blossoms on the air.

I set our sail to seek them,
    But she, my Love, drew back :—
" Not yet ; the night is chilly,
    I fear that unknown track."

C

So home we sailed at twilight,
　To the familiar shore ;
Turned from the golden glory,
　To live the old life o'er.

We'll make no farther ventures—
　For timid is my Love—
Until fresh sailing orders
　Are sent us from above :

Then past the deep mid-ocean
　'Twixt life and life we'll steer
To land on happier islands
　Than those we dreamed of here.

A WEED.

How shall a little weed grow
   That has no sun ?
Rains fall and north winds blow—
   What shall be done ?

Out come some little pale leaves
   At the spring's call,
But the harsh north winds blow,
   And the sad rains fall.

Wouldst try to keep it warm
   With fickle breath ?
He must, who would give life,
   Be Lord of death.

Some day you forget the weed—
    Man's thoughts are brief—
And your coldness steals like frost
    Through each pale leaf,

Till the weed shrinks back to die
    On kinder sod ;
Shall a life which found no sun,
    In death find God ?

THROUGH A WINDOW.

I LIE here at rest in my chamber,
   And look through the window again,
With eyes that are changed since the old time
   And the sting of an exquisite pain.

'Tis not much that I see for a picture,
   Through boughs that are green with spring—
A barn grown gray with lichen,
   And above it a bird on the wing ;

Or, lifting my head a thought higher,
   Some hills and a village I know,
And over it all the blue heaven,
   With a white cloud floating below.

Ah, once the roof was a prison—
  My mind and the sky were free,
My thoughts with the birds went flying,
  And my hopes were a heaven to me.

Now I come from the limitless distance
  Where I followed my youth's wild will,
Where they press the wine of delusion
  That you drink and are thirsty still :

And I know why the bird with the spring time
  To the gnarled old tree comes back—
He has tried the south and the summer,
  He has felt what the sweet things lack.

So I come with a sad contentment,
  With eyes that are changed I see :
The roof means peace, not a prison,
  And heaven smiles down on me.

THE HOUSE OF DEATH.

Not a hand has lifted the latchet
    Since she went out of the door—
No footstep shall cross the threshold
    Since she can come in no more.

There is rust upon locks and hinges,
    And mold and blight on the walls,
And silence faints in the chambers,
    And darkness waits in the halls—

Waits as all things have waited
    Since she went, that day of spring,
Borne in her pallid splendour
    To dwell in the Court of the King:

With lilies on brow and bosom,
  With robes of silken sheen,
And her wonderful, frozen beauty
  The lilies and silk between.

Red roses she left behind her,
  But they died long, long ago—
'Twas the odorous ghost of a blossom
  That seemed through the dusk to glow.

The garments she left mock the shadows
  With hints of womanly grace,
And her image swims in the mirror
  That was so used to her face.

The birds make insolent music
  Where the sunshine riots outside,
And the winds are merry and wanton
  With the summer's pomp and pride.

But into this desolate mansion,
　Where Love has closed the door,
Nor sunshine nor summer shall enter,
　Since she can come in no more.

WAITING.

"I'M waiting for my darling,
  Here, sitting by the sea,
Whom never any ship that sails
  Brings home again to me.

"Oh, sailor ! have you seen her?
  You'd know her by her eyes—
No other are so tender,
  So full of glad surprise."

"Yes, I have seen your darling—
  A fair wind never fails
To waft the good ship unto
  The shore for which she sails.

" King Death they call the Captain—
  His crew a spectral band—
He steers with pennons flying
  Toward a far-off land.

" No other ship goes thither,
  And back across that main
The passengers he carries
  He never brings again."

A LIFE'S LOSS.

Do you remember the summer day
   You found me down by the ruined mill?
The skies were blue, and the waters bright,
   And shadows glanced on the windy hill,
           And the stream moaned on.

You sat by my side on the moss-grown log,
   Where one I loved last night had stood—
I heard his voice, like an undertone,
   While you talked to me in that solitude,
           And the stream moaned on.

You did not tell me your heart was mine—
　You only said that my face was fair,
That silks and satins should robe my form,
　And jewels should flash among my hair,
　　　　　And the stream moaned on.

You did not ask me to give you love—
　You did not touch my lips or brow—
Contented you were with my plighted troth,
　And never a kiss to seal the vow,
　　　　　And the stream moaned on.

You went away with that careless air,
　And smiled as you uttered your light good-bye,
But the wind stole down from the frowning hill,
　And stood at my side with a gasping sigh,
　　　　　And the stream moaned on.

You remember the pomp of our bridal morn—
 The jewels that mocked the bright sunshine—
The rustling silks—the ringing mirth—
 The flush of roses—the flow of wine—
   While the crowd looked on ?

I saw a sight they did not see—
 A guest they knew not of was there—
Heart of my heart ! he came to mock
 My bridal vows with his pale despair,
   And my soul moaned on.

You got, that day, what you bargained for—
 My hair to braid your jewels in,
My form to deck with your silken robes,
 My face to show to your haughty kin,
   But my soul moaned on.

Talk not of love !—You come too late—
  You cannot dispel my heart's eclipse—
Where your image should be a corpse lies shrined,
  And no voice comes from the death-cold lips,
        Though my soul moans on.

Some summer day I shall wander down
  Where the waters flow by the ruined mill—
Where the shadows come, and the shadows go,
  There at the foot of the windy hill,
        And the stream moans on.

You will find me there, 'neath the whispering wave,
  Colder and stiller than ever before—
The dreams I dreamed and the hopes I hoped
  Will be hushed to silence for evermore—
        Though the stream moan on.

ALONE BY THE BAY.

HE is gone.   O my heart, he is gone ;
　And the sea remains and the sky,
And the skiffs flit in and out,
　And the white-winged yachts go by :

The waves run purple and green,
　And the sunshine glints and glows,
And freshly across the bay
　The breath of the morning blows.

I liked it better last night,
　When the dark shut down on the main,
And the phantom fleet lay still
　And I heard the waves complain :

For the sadness that dwells in my heart,
  And the rune of their endless woe—
Their longing, and void, and despair—
  Kept time in their ebb and flow.

AFTER THE MOUNTAINS.

(TO L. C. B.)

In my dreams I see the hilltops—
  Where the cloudy pathways led
You and I have trod together
  In the days that now are dead—

Still I see their shining splendours
  Height on height before me rise,
And the radiance of their glory
  Streams across my half-shut eyes.

In my dreams you are beside me—
  Still I hear your tender tone,
While your soft eyes beam upon me,
  And I am no more alone,

For with memories I am haunted,
   Till the silence seems to beat
With your music of your talking
   And the coming of your feet.

Turn towards me, from the distance,
   Sweetest heart, your gentle eyes ;
Though far-off I sure shall see them—
   Stars are farther in the skies.

AT ETRETAT.

.

THE ocean beats against the stern, dumb shore
  The stormy passion of its mighty heart—
The sky where no stars shine is black above,
  And thou and I sit from the world apart.

We two, with lives no star of hope makes bright—
  Whom bliss forgets, and joy no longer mocks—
Hark to the wind's wild cry, the sea's complaint,
  And break with wind and sea against the rocks.

Sore-wounded, hurled on the dark shore of Fate,
  We stretch out helpless hands, and cry in vain—
Our joy went forth, white-sailed, at dawn of day,
  To-night is pitiless for all our pain.

We are not glad of any morn to come,

    Since that winged joy we never more shall see—

But in the passion of the winds and waves

    Something there seems akin to thee and me.

They call !   Shall we not go, out on that tide,

    To touch, perchance, some shore where tempests

      cease,

Where no wind blows, and storm-torn souls forget

    Their past disasters in that utmost peace ?

A PROBLEM.

My darling has a merry eye,
  And voice like silver bells :
How shall I win her, prithee, say—
  By what magic spells ?

If I frown she shakes her head,
  If I weep she smiles ;
Time would fail me to recount
  All her wilful wiles.

She flouts me so—she stings me so—
  Yet will not let me stir—
In vain I try to pass her by,
  My little chestnut bur.

When I yield to every whim
    She straight begins to pout :
Teach me how to read my love,
    How to find her out !

For flowers she gives me thistle blooms—
    Her turtle doves are crows—
I am the groaning weather-vane,
    And she the wind that blows.

My little love ! My teasing love !
    Was woman made for man—
A rose that blossomed from his side ?
    Believe it—those who can.

MY CAPTIVE.

I CAUGHT a little bird, and I shut him in a cage,
  And I said, " Now, my pet, I love thee dearly.
Fold thy bright wings, nor let thy fancy range :
  Thou'rt mine own, so sing, I pray thee, cheerly."

But O, the little bird, he fluttered still his wings,
  And with bright, wild eyes he never ceased to
    watch me,
And I only heard him say, " 'Tis a free heart that
    sings—
Open my door, and I'll sing till you catch me."

I brought him dainty food, and I soothed him long
    and well,
    But the timid little heart ceased not to tremble :
I decked his cage with flowers, with leaves I wrought
    a spell,
    By such fond device his capture to dissemble.

But still he missed above him the far and shining sky,
    And still he missed the free winds blowing ;
He beat his little wings, for he had no space to fly,
    And his bright, wild eyes like twin stars were
    glowing.

And I heard his little heart, as it throbbed so loud
    and fast,
    And my love and my pity wrought together,
Till I opened wide his door, and I said, " Thy thral-
    dom's past,
    Fly away, bright wings, and seek the summer weather."

But now I think he loves me, since I have made him
    free—
  For, oftentimes, at daybreak or at gloaming,
I think I hear a song that seems to be for me—
  "Throw wide the door, to keep a heart from
    roaming."

THE SINGER.

WITHIN the crimson gloom
Of that dim, shaded room
  I heard a singer sing :

She sang of life and death,
Of joys that end with breath,
  And joys the end doth bring ;

Of passion's bitter pain,
And memory's tears, like rain
  That will not cease to flow ;

Of the deep grave's delights,
Where through long days and nights
    They hear the green things grow—

Cool-rooted flowers that come
So near to that still home,
    Their ways the dead must know—

And shivers in the grass,
When winds of summer pass,
    And whisper as they go

Of the mad life above,
Where men like masquers move ;
    Or are they ghosts—who knows?—

Sad ghosts who cannot die,
And watch slow years go by
    Amid those painted shows—

Who knows ?   For on her tongue
What never may be sung
  Seemed trembling ; and we wait

To catch the strain complete,
More full, but not more sweet,
  Beyond the golden gate.

HOW LONG?

IF on my grave the summer grass were growing,
Or heedless winter winds across it blowing,
Through joyous June, or desolate December,
How long, sweetheart, how long would you remember—
    How long, dear love, how long?

For brightest eyes would open to the summer,
And sweetest smiles would greet the sweet new-comer,
And on young lips grow kisses for the taking,
When all the summer buds to bloom are breaking—
    How long, dear love, how long?

To the dim land where sad-eyed ghosts walk only,

Where lips are cold, and waiting hearts are lonely,

I would not call you from your youth's warm blisses,

Fill up your glass and crown it with new kisses—

    How long, dear love, how long?

Too gay in June you might be to regret me,

And living lips might woo you to forget me ;

But ah, sweetheart, I think you would remember

When winds were weary in your life's December—

    So long, dear love, so long.

THE SONG OF A SUMMER.

I PLUCKED an apple from off a tree,
Golden and rosy and fair to see—
The sunshine had fed it with warmth and light,
The dews had freshened it night by night,
And high on the topmost bough it grew,
Where the winds of Heaven about it blew,
And while the mornings were soft and young
The wild birds circled, and soared, and sung—
There, in the storm and calm and shine,
It ripened and brightened, this apple of mine,
Till the day I plucked it from off the tree
Golden and rosy and fair to see.

How could I guess 'neath that daintiest rind
That the core of sweetness I hoped to find—
The innermost, hidden heart of the bliss
Which dews and winds and the sunshine's kiss
Had tended and fostered by day and night—
Was black with mildew, and bitter with blight;
Golden and rosy and fair of skin,
Nothing but ashes and ruin within !
Ah, never again, with toil and pain,
Will I strive the topmost bough to gain—
Though its wind-swung apples are fair to see,
On a lower branch is the fruit for me.

IF.

WHAT had I been, lost Love, if you had loved me?
  A woman smiling as the smiling May—
As gay of heart as birds that carol gaily
  Their sweet young songs to usher in the day—

As ardent as the skies that brood and brighten
  O'er the warm fields in summer's happy prime—
As tender as the veiling grace that softens
  The harshest shapes in twilight's tender time.

Like the soft dusk I would have veiled your harshness
  With tendernesses that were not your due—
Your very faults had blossomed into virtues
  Had you known how to love me and be true.

It had been well for you—for me how blessed—
　But shall we ask the wind to blow for aye
From one same quarter, keep at full for ever
　The white moon smiling in a changeless sky?

Change is the law of wind and moon and lover—
　And yet I think, lost Love, had you been true,
Some golden fruits had ripened for your plucking,
　You will not find in gardens that are new.

FIAT JUSTITIA.

YES, all is ended now, for I have weighed thee—
  Weighed the light love that has been held so dear—
Weighed word, and look, and smile that have betrayed
    thee,
  The careless grace that was not worth a tear.

Holding these scales, I marvel at the anguish
  For thing so slight that long my heart has torn—
For God's great sun the prisoner's eyes might languish,
  Not for a torch by some chance passer borne.

I do not blame thee for thy heedless playing
  On the strong chords whose answer was so full—
Do children care, through daisied meadows straying,
  What hap befalls the blossoms that they pull?

Go on, gay trifler !   Take thy childish pleasure—

On thee, for thee, may summer always shine—

Too stern were Justice should she seek to measure

Thy fitful love by the strong pain of mine.

AT THE LAST.

Come once, just once, dear Love, when I am dead—
    Ah, God ! I would it were this hour, to-night—
And look your last upon the frozen face
    That was to you a summer's brief delight.

The silent lips will not entreat you then,
    Nor the eyes vex you with unwelcome tears ;
The low, sad voice will utter no complaint,
    Nor the heart tremble with its restless fears.

I shall be still—you will forgive me then
    For all that I have been, or failed to be ;
Say, as you look, " Poor heart, she loved me well,
    No other love will be so true to me."

Then bend and kiss the lips that will not speak—
One little kiss for all the dear, dead days—
Say once, "God rest her soul!" then go in peace,
No haunting ghost shall meet you in your ways.

WHAT SHE SAID IN HER TOMB.

Now at last I lie asleep
  Where no morrows break—
Why take heed to tread so soft ?
  Fear you lest I wake ?

Time there was when I was red
  As a rose in June
With the kisses of your lips—
  Ah, they failed me soon.

Now they would not warm my mouth
  Though they fell like rain ;
I am marble, dear, and they
  Marble cannot stain.

Ah, if you had loved me more,
   Been content to wait,
Some time you had found the key
   To Love's inmost gate.

Why, indeed, should any man
   Wait for autumn days,
When the present summer wooes
   To her rosy ways?

Only—now I lie here dead,
   I shall not awake,
And you need not softly tread
   For my deaf ears' sake.

A SUMMER'S GHOST.

In that old summer can you still recall
　The pomp wherewith the strong sun rose and set,
How bright the moon shone on the shining fields,
　What wild, sweet blossoms with the dew were wet ?

Can you still hear the merry robins sing,
　And see the brave red lilies gleam and glow,
The waiting wealth of bloom, the reckless bees
　That woo their wild-flower loves, and sting, and go?

Can you still hear the waves that round the shore
　Broke in soft joy and told delusive tales—
" We go, but we return ; Love comes and goes ;
　And eyes that watch see homeward-faring sails."

"' 'Twas thus in other seasons?" Ah, may be !
But *I* forget them, and remember this—
A brief, warm season, and a fond, brief love,
And cold, white winter after bloom and bliss.

BEAUTY FOR ASHES.

BEAUTY for ashes thou hast brought me, dear !
  A time there was when all my soul lay waste,
As ere the dawn the earth lies dark and drear,
  Whereto the golden feet of morn make haste.

Like morn thou camest, blessings in thy hands,
  And gracious pity round thine ardent mouth—
Like dews of morning upon waiting lands,
  Thy tender tears refreshed my spirit's drouth.

To-day is calm.   Far off the tempest raves
  That long ago swept dead men to the shore—
I can forget the wildness of the waves,
  Against my hopes and me they break no more.

White butterflies flit shining in the sun—
 Red roses burst to bloom upon the tree—
Birds call to birds till the glad day is done,
 The day of beauty thou hast brought to me.

Shall I forget, O gentle heart and true,
 How thy fair dawn has risen on my night—
Turned dark to day all golden through and through—
 From soil of grief won bloom of new delight.

TO MY HEART.

In thy long, lonely times, poor aching heart !
When days are slow, and silent nights are sad,
Take cheer, weak heart, remember and be glad,
              For some one loved thee :

Some one, indeed, who cared for fading face,
For time-touched hair, and weary-falling arm,
And in thy very sadness found a charm
              To make him love thee.

God knows thy days are desolate, poor heart !
As thou dost sit alone, and dumbly wait
For what comes not, or comes, alas, too late,
              But some one loved thee.

Take cheer, poor heart, remembering what he said,
And how of thy lost youth he missed no grace,
But saw some subtler beauty in thy face,
             So well he loved thee.

It may be, on Time's farther shore, the dead
Love the sweet shades of those they missed on this,
And dream, in heavenly rest, of earth's lost bliss—
             So he shall love thee.

Till then take cheer, poor, silent, aching heart ;
Content thee with the face he once found fair,
Mourn not for fading bloom, or time-touched hair,
             Since he hath loved thee.

"LOVER AND FRIEND HAST THOU PUT FAR FROM ME."

(PSALM LXXXVIII. 18.)

I HEAR the soft September rain entone,
 And cheerful crickets chirping in the grass,
I bow my head—I who am all alone—
 The light winds see, and shiver as they pass.

No other thing is so bereft as I—
 The rain-drops fall, and mingle as they fall ;
The chirping cricket knows his neighbour nigh ;
 Leaves sway responsive to the light wind's call : ·

But Friend and Lover Thou hast put afar,
  And left me only Thy great, solemn sky—
I try to pierce beyond the farthest star
  To search Thee out, and find Thee ere I die :

But dim my vision is, or Thou dost hide
  Thy sacred splendour from my yearning eyes—
Be pitiful, O God, and open wide
  To me, bereft, Thy heavenly Paradise.

Give me one glimpse of that sweet, far-off rest,
  Then I can bear Earth's solitude again—
My soul returning from that Heavenly quest
  Shall smile, triumphant, at each transient pain.

Nor would I vex my heart with grief or strife,
  Though Friend and Lover Thou hast put afar,
If I could see, through my worn tent of life,
  The steadfast shining of Thy morning star.

F

THERE.

Do any hearts ache there, beyond the peaceful river?
　Do fond souls wait, with longing in their eyes,
For those who come not, will not come, for ever—
　For some wild hope whose dawn will never rise?

Do any love there still, beyond the silent river,
　The ones they loved in vain, this side its flow?
Does the old pain make their heart-strings ache and
　　quiver?
　I shall go home, some day, go home and know.

The hilltops are bright there, beyond the shining river,
　And the long, glad day, it never turns to night—
They must be blest, indeed, to bear the light for ever,
　Grief longs for darkness to hide its tears from sight.

Are tears turned to smiling, beyond the blessed river,
    And mortal pain and passion drowned in its flow?
Then all we who sit on its hither bank and shiver,
    Let us rejoice—we shall go home and know.

HER WINDOW.

Out of her window, that morn of grace,
She leaned her radiant, beautiful face—
The sun, ashamed, went into a cloud,
But glad of the dawning the birds sang loud.

A laggard went up the garden walk,
And lingered to hear the murmuring talk
Of flower, and bee, and every comer
That fluttered along in front of the summer.

He quaffed the wine of the morning air,
And felt with a thrill that the day was fair—
Then he raised his eyes to her window's height,
" Ah me," he said, " but the sun is bright ! "

ROSES.

HAROLD, on a summer day,
   Gave me roses for my hair—
Roses red, and roses white,
   As if pale with Love's despair :

White ones for my brow, he said—
   Red to blush beside my cheek—
And a bud to whisper me
   Something that he dared not speak.

Ah, that summer day is fled,
   And its brightness comes not back ;
Harold's roses something held
   Other roses seem to lack.

Blossoms bloom along my path,
  Red and white as those were then;
But such words as Harold spoke
  I shall never hear again.

LOVE'S LAND.

" In the south is Love's land,
　Where the roses blow
　Where the summer lingers,
　　Fearless of the snow.
'There no winter chills it,
　So its life is long—
Gentle breezes fan it,
　　Age but makes it strong."

" Nay, fresh roses wither
　　Where the sun is hot—
Not in torrid regions
　　Blooms forget-me-not.
Love's a tender blossom,
　　Which the winter chills,
But the eager summer
　　Kisses it and kills."

LOOKING BACK.

I MAY live long, but some old days
   Of dear, deep joy akin to pain,
Some suns that set on woodland ways
   Will never rise for me again :
By shining sea, and glad, green shore
   That frolic waves ran home to kiss,
Some words I heard that never more
   Will thrill me with their mystic bliss.

O love ! still throbs your living heart—
   You have not crossed death's sullen tide—
A deeper deep holds us apart :
   We were more near if you had died—

If you had died in those old days
  When light was on the shining sea,
And all the fragrant woodland ways
  Were paths of hope for you and me.

Dead leaves are in those woodland ways—
  Cold are the lips that used to kiss:
'Twere idle to recall those days,
  Or sigh for all that vanished bliss.
Do you still wear your old-time grace,
  And charm new loves with ancient wiles?
Could I but watch your faithless face,
  I'd know the meaning of your smiles.

THE SPRING IS LATE.

SHE stood alone amid the April fields—
  Brown, sodden fields, all desolate and bare—
" The spring is late," she said—" the faithless spring,
  That should have come to make the meadows fair.

" Their sweet South left too soon, among the trees
  The birds, bewildered, flutter to and fro ;
For them no green boughs wait—their memories
  Of last year's April had deceived them so.

" From 'neath a sheltering pine some tender buds
  Looked out, and saw the hollows filled with snow ;
On such a frozen world they closed their eyes ;—
  When spring is cold, how can the blossoms blow ? "

She watched the homeless birds, the slow, sad spring,
  The barren fields, and shivering, naked trees :
" Thus God has dealt with me, his child," she said—
  " I wait my spring time, and am cold like these.

" To them will come the fulness of their time ;
  Their spring, though late, will make the meadows
    fair ;
Shall I, who wait like them, like them be blessed ?
  I am His own—doth not my Father care ? "

A SONG IN THE WOOD.

I FOUND a shy little violet root
    Half hid in the woods, on a day of spring,
And a bird flew over, and looked at it, too,
    And for joy, as he looked, began to sing.

The sky was the tenderest blue above—
    And the flower like a bit of the sky below ;
And between them the wonderful winds of God
    On heavenly errands went to and fro.

Away from the summer, and out of the South
    The bird had followed an instinct true,
As out from the brown and desolate sod
    Stepped the shy little blossom, with eyes of blue.

And he sang to her, in the young spring day,
    Of all the joy in the world astir :
And her beauty and fragrance answered him,
    While the spring and he bent over her.

SONNETS.

THE NEW DAY.

WHEN the great sun sets the glad east aflame
  The lingering stars are swiftly put to flight,
  For day, triumphant, overthrows the night
And mocks the lights that twinkled till he came—
The waning moon retires in sudden shame,
  And all the air, from roseate height to height,
  Quivers with wings of birds that take the light
With jubilant music of one tender name.

So Thou hast risen, now, who art my day,
And every lesser light has ceased to shine—
  Pale stars confronted by this dawn of thine
  Like night and gloom and grief have passed away;
And yet my bliss I fear to call it mine
  Lest fresh foes lurk with unforeseen dismay.

ONE DREAD.

No depth, dear Love, for thee is too profound,
　There is no farthest height thou may'st not dare,
　Nor shall thy wings fail in the upper air :
In funeral robes and wreaths my past lies wound :
No ancient strain assails me with its sound
　Hearing thy voice ; no former joy seems fair,
　Since now one only thing could bring despair,
One grief, like compassing seas, my life surround.
　One only terror in my way be met,
One great eclipse change my glad day to night,
One phantom only turn from red to white
　The lips whereon thy lips have once been set :
Thou knowest well, dear Love, what that must be—
The dread of some dark day unshared by thee.

AFAR.

WHERE Thou art not no day holds light for me :
   The brightest noontide turns to midnight deep,
   Where no bird sings and awesome shadows creep—-
Persistent ghosts that hold my memory,
And walk where joy and hope once walked with Thee,
   And in thy place their lonesome vigil keep,
   Sad ghosts that haunt the inmost ways of sleep—
Ghosts whom no kindly morning makes to flee.

   Their tireless footsteps never more will cease—-
Like crownless queens they tread their ancient ways,
These phantoms of old dreams, and vanished days,
   And mock my poor endeavours after peace :
Too long this arctic night, too keen its cold—
Come back, strong sun, and warm me as of old.

LAST YEAR.

I.

You thought, O Love, you loved me then, I know—
For that I bless you, now when Love is cold,
Remembering how warm the tale you told,
When winds of autumn fitfully did blow,
And, by the sea's perpetual ebb and flow,
We wandered on together to behold
Noon's radiant splendour, or the sunset's gold,
Or beauty of still nights when moons hung low.
Your voice grew tender as you called my name;
I heard that voice to-day—was it the same?—
The old time's music trembles in it yet;
Your touch thrilled through me like a sudden flame,
And then a sweet and subtle madness came
And lips, cold now, my lips had quickly met.

II.

Ah Love, you must remember, though, to-day,
  There is no spell to charm you in the past—
  So dear the dream was that it could not last :
Full soon our pleasant skies were changed to gray,
The sun turned from our barren land away,
  And all the leaves swept by us on the blast,
  And all our hopes to that wild wind were cast—
For dead Love's soul there is no place to pray.
But still the old time lives in each our thought—
  In our regretful dreams the old suns rise,
And, from their shining, memory hath caught
  Some lingering glory of the glad surprise
When Love rose on us like the sun, and brought
  Our hearts their morning, under Last Year's skies.

FIRST LOVE.

TIME was you heard the music of a sigh,

    And Love awoke, and with it Song was born--

    Song glad as young birds carol in the morn,

And tender as the blue and brooding sky,

When all the earth feels spring's warm witchery,

    And with fresh flowers her bosom doth adorn--

    Then lovers love, and cannot love forlorn,

And Love is of the gods and cannot die.

In after years may come some wildering light—

    Some sweet delusion followed for a space—

Such fitful fireflies but flash through the night,

    And fade before the shining of that face

Which shines upon you still, in Death's despite,

    Whose steadfast beauty lights till death your days.

LOVE'S FORGIVENESS.

I DO forgive you for the pain I bear,
   Though bitter pain is mingled with my bliss,
   And still I think, though thrilling to your kiss—
" He found that other woman much more fair ! "
I read your words, and see depicted there
   Another love—how warm it was to this !—
   How surely, loving, I must always miss
The glory that another used to wear !
Yet I forgive you, dear, and bow my head
   To Destiny, my master and your own—
He sets the way wherein my feet must tread,
   And if he give me nothing quite mine own
I think some day my heart, so sore bested,
   Will rest most quietly, and turn to stone.

IN TIME TO COME.

THE time will come, full soon, I shall be gone
   And you sit silent in the silent place,
   With the sad autumn sunlight on your face :
Remembering the loves that were your own,
Haunted, perchance, by some familiar tone,
   You will grow weary then for the dead days,
   And mindful of their sweet and bitter ways,
Though passion into memory shall have grown—
Then shall I, with your other ghosts, draw nigh,
   And whisper, as I pass, some former word,
Some old endearment known in days gone by,
   Some tenderness that once your pulses stirred—
Which was it spoke to you, the wind or I,
I think you, musing, scarcely will have heard.

A SUMMER'S GROWTH.

FAIR was the flower which proffers now its fruit—

The bud began to swell 'neath spring's soft dew,

And tenderly the winds of summer blew

To foster it, and great, strong suns were mute

As through its veins warm life began to shoot,

And it put on, each day, some beauty new;

And all the fairer, as I think, it grew

Because the streams were tears about its root.

But now our fruit hangs well within our reach,

And this, indeed, is time for gathering:

It hath the bloom of summer-tinted peach;

Each charm it hath that any man could sing;

Yet we who taste it whisper, each to each,

" Not sweet but very bitter is this thing!"

A MADRIGAL.

Love is a day, Sweetheart, shining and bright :
It hath its rose-dawn ere the morning light—
Its glow and glory of the sudden sun—
Its noontide heat as the swift hours wear on—
Its fall of dew, and silver-lighted night—
Love is a day, Sweetheart, shining and bright.

Love is a year, Beloved, bitter and brief :
It hath its spring of bud, and bloom, and leaf—
Its summer burning from the fervid south
Till all the fields lie parched and faint with drouth—

Its autumn, when the leaves sweep down the gale,

When skies are gray, and heart and spirit fail—

Its winter white with snow, more white with grief—

Love is a year, Beloved, bitter and brief.

Love is a life, Sweetheart, ending in death :

Is it worth while to mourn its fleeting breath—

Light-footed youth, or sad, forecasting prime,

Joy of young hope, or grief of later time ?

What pain or pleasure stays its parting breath ?—

Love is a life, Sweetheart, ending in death.

QUESTION.

Dear and blessed dead ones, can you look and listen
  To the sighing and the moaning down here below?
Does it make a discord in the hymns of Heaven—
  The discord that jangles in the life you used to
    know?

When we pray our prayers to the great God above you,
  Does the echo of our praying ever glance aside your
    way?
Do you know the thing we ask for, and wish that you
    could give it—
  You whose hearts ached with wishing, in your own
    little day?

Are your ears deaf with praises, you blessed dead
of Heaven,
And your eyes blind with glory, that you cannot
see our pain ?
If you saw, if you heard, you would weep among the
angels,
And the praises and the glory would be for you in
vain.

Yet He listens to our praying, the great God of pity,
As He fills with pain the measure of our Life's little
day—
Could He bear to sit and shine there, on His white
throne in Heaven,
But that He sees the end, while we only see the
way ?

ALIEN WATERS.

I WANDERED long beside the alien waters,
    For summer suns were warm, and winds were
      dead—
Fields, fair as hope, were stretching on before me,
    Forbidden paths were pleasant to my tread.

From boughs that hung between me and the heavens
    I gathered summer fruitage red and gold—
For me the idle singers sang of pleasure;
    My days went by like stories that are told.

On my rose-tree grew roses for my plucking,
    As red as love, or pale as tender pain—
I found no thorns to vex me in my garlands;
    Each day was good, and no rose bloomed in vain.

Sometimes I danced, as in a dream, to music,
  And kept quick time with many flying feet,
And someone praised me in the music's pauses,
  And very young was life, and love was sweet.

How could I listen to the low voice calling—
  " Come hither, leave thy music and thy mirth ? "
How could I stop to hear of far-off Heaven ?—
  I lived and loved, and was a child of earth.

Then came a hand and took away my treasures,
  Dimmed my fine gold, cut my fair rose-tree down,
Changed my dance music into notes of wailing,
  Quenched the bright day, and turned my green
    fields brown.

Till, walking lonely through the empty places
  Where Love and I no more kept holiday,
My sad eyes, growing wonted to the darkness,
  Beheld a new light shining far away ;

And I could bear my hopes should lie around me
  Dead like my roses, fallen before their time,
For well I knew some tender spring would raise them
  To brighter blooming in a far-off. clime.

I FAIN WOULD GO.

Away from carking care,
From passion and despair,
From hopes that but delude,
And blasts that are too rude—
From friendships that betray,
And joys that pass away,
And love that turns to hate
In hearts left desolate,
                    I fain would go.

From weary days and nights,
And ghosts of lost delights—

Fair phantoms of dead days,
That wander through old ways—
From parting's bitter pain,
And meeting's transient gain,
And death that mocks us so
With glad life's overthrow
              I fain would go.

To some fair land and far
Where all my lost ones are,
Where smiles shall bloom anew,
And friendship shall be true,
Where falls no weary night,
Since God himself is light—
Across the soundless sea
To that far land, and free,
              I fain would go.

AD TE DOMINE.

O Thou who sendest dewdrops to the garden,
    Until each fragrant bud receives its own,
Canst Thou not look on human hearts and pardon
    To waiting loneliness its bitter moan?

The flowers can drink the dawn—it hastens to them ;
    But hearts athirst wait sadly for their hour,
For the sweet gift that may perchance undo them—
    Too fatal sweet a dew for human flower.

Wilt Thou not, then, give love to bless the loving—
    Forgive the human heart that seeks its lord,
And drown in rapture earthly disapproving—
    Blend all life's discords in one grand accord?

H

SELFISH PRAYER.

How we, poor players on Life's little stage,
Thrust blindly at each other in our rage,
Quarrel and fret yet rashly dare to pray
To God to help us in our selfish way !

We think to move Him with our prayer and praise
To serve our needs—as in the old Greek days
Their gods came down and mingled in the fight,
With mightier arms the flying foe to smite.

The laughter of those gods pealed down to men,
For heaven was but earth's upper storey, then,
Where goddesses about an apple strove,
And the high gods fell humanly in love.

SELFISH PRAYER.

We own a God whose presence fills the sky—
Whose sleepless eyes behold the worlds roll by—
Whose faithful memory numbers one by one,
The sons of men, and calls them each His son.

SOMEBODY'S CHILD.

Just a picture of somebody's child—
  Sweet face set in its golden hair,
Violet eyes, and cheeks of rose,
  Rounded chin with a dimple there ;

Tender eyes where the shadows sleep,
  Lit from within by a secret ray ;
Tender eyes that will shine like stars
  When love and womanhood come this way ;

Scarlet lips with a story to tell—
  Blessed be he who shall find it out,
Who shall learn the eyes' deep secret well,
  And read the heart with never a doubt !

Then you will tremble, scarlet lips ;
　Then you will crimson, loveliest cheeks ;
Eyes will brighten and blushes will burn
　When the one true lover bends and speaks.

But she's only a child now, as you see,
　Only a child in her careless grace ;
When love and womanhood come this way
　Will anything sadden the flower-like face ?

IF I COULD KEEP HER SO.

Just a little baby, lying in my arms—
Would that I could keep you, with your baby charms ;
Helpless, clinging fingers, downy, golden hair,
Where the sunshine lingers, caught from otherwhere ;
Blue eyes asking questions, lips that cannot speak,
Roly-poly shoulders, dimple in your cheek ;
Dainty little blossom in a world of woe,
Thus I fain would keep you, for I love you so.

Roguish little damsel, scarcely six years old—
Feet that never weary, hair of deeper gold ;
Restless, busy fingers all the time at play ;
Tongue that never ceases talking all the day ;

Blue eyes learning wonders of the world about,
Here you come to tell them—what an eager shout !—
Winsome little damsel, all the neighbours know ;
Thus I long to keep you, for I love you so.

Sober little schoolgirl, with your strap of books,
And such grave importance in your puzzled looks ;
Solving weary problems, poring over sums,
Yet with tooth for sponge-cake and for sugar-plums ;
Reading books of romance in your bed at night,
Waking up to study with the morning light ;
Anxious as to ribbons, deft to tie a bow,
Full of contradictions—I would keep you so.

Sweet and thoughtful maiden, sitting by my side,
All the world's before you, and the world is wide ;
Hearts are there for winning, hearts are there to break,
Has your own, shy maiden, just begun to wake ?

Is that rose of dawning glowing on your cheek
Telling us in blushes what you will not speak ?
Shy and tender maiden, I would fain forego
All the golden future, just to keep you so.

Ah ! the listening angels saw that she was fair,
Ripe for rare unfolding in the upper air ;
Now the rose of dawning turns to lily white,
And the close-shut eyelids veil the eyes from sight ;
All the past I summon as I kiss her brow—
Babe, and child, and maiden, all are with me now.
Though my heart is breaking, yet God's love I know—
Safe among the angels, I would keep her so.

ANNIE'S DAUGHTER.

THE lingering charm of a dream that has fled,
The rose's breath when the rose is dead,
The echo that lives when the tune is done,
The sunset glories that follow the sun,
Everything tender and everything fair
That was, and is not, and yet is there—
I think of them all when I look in these eyes,
And see the old smile to the young lips rise.

I remember the lilacs all purple and white,
And the turf at the feet of my heart's delight,
Sprinkled with daisies and violets sweet—
Daintiest floor for the daintiest feet—

And the face that was fond and foolish and fair,

And the golden grace of the floating hair,

And the lips where the glad smiles came and went,

And the lashes that shaded the eyes' content:

I remember the pledge of the red young lips,

And the shy soft touch of the finger-tips,

And the kisses I stole, and the words we spoke,

And the ring I gave, and the coin we broke,

And the love that never should change or fail

Though the earth stood still or the stars turned
    pale ;

And again I stand, when I see these eyes,

A glad young fool, in my Paradise.

For the earth and the stars remained as of old

But the love that had been so warm grew cold :

Was it she ?   Was it I ?   I don't remember :

Then it was June—it is now December.

But again I dream the old dream over,

My Annie is young, and I am her lover,

When I look in this Annie's gentle eyes,

And see the old smile to the young lips rise.

MY BOY.

I HAD a little bird once,
   But he has flown away;
I had a little boy once,
   But, ah ! he did not stay.

What do they up in heaven,
   That bird and boy should fly,
And leave my home so empty,
   To seek the far-off sky ?

What do they up in heaven ?
   Perchance the angels sing ;
And when they heard that music
   My bird and boy took wing.

The heavenly flowers bloom always,
   The skies are always bright,
And all the little children
   Play there from morn till night.

But do they never weary
   And long to go to rest,
Like little human children
   Upon a mother's breast?

My home and arms are empty,
   My longing heart is sore,
Since they who sought the summer
   Come back to me no more.

How softly falls the twilight—
   The sunset fires are out—
A wind that comes from heaven
   Blows slowly round about.

I close my eyes and listen,
    And presently I hear
A small voice through the darkness
    Sigh, " Mother, I am near.

" Come, take me in, dear mother,
    And rock me as of old ;
I used to be so happy
    Within your tender hold !

" There sorrow cannot find me,
    And pain shall pass me by—
When you enfold who love me
    No danger can come nigh.

" So safe I was in heaven !
    So bright the shining days !
But from afar your weeping
    Disturbed the hymns of praise ;

" Till the dear Lord and gentle
Sent me to soothe your pain ;
And if you fain would keep me
He bids me to remain."

I kissed his tender eyelids,
I laid him on my heart ;
And yet when came the dawning,
I prayed him to depart.

I feared the unknown future—
I feared the paths untried—
How dared I keep my darling
When heaven was opened wide ?

But yet my heart is lonely
Since boy and bird have fled ;
I hear the silence only,
And wish that I were dead.

LIKE A CHILD.

PLAYING there in the sun,
   Chasing the butterflies,
Catching his golden toy,
   Holding it fast till it dies ;
Singing to match the birds,
   Calling the robins at will,
Glancing here and there,
   Never a moment still—
            Like a child.

Going to school at last,
   Learning to read and write,
Puzzled over his slate,
   Busy from morn till night,

Striving to win a prize,
  Careless when it is won,
Finding his joy in the strife,
  Not in the thing that's done :

Busy in eager trade,
  Buying and selling again,
Chasing a golden prize,
  Glad of a transient gain ;
Always beginning anew
  Never the long task done,
Just as it used to be—
  With the butterfly in the sun.

Seeking a woman's heart,
  Winning it for his own,
Then, too busy for love,
  Letting it turn to stone.

I

Sure of his plighted truth
  What more had a wife to ask ?
Is he not doing for her
  Each day his daily task ?

A child, to pine and complain !
  A child, to grow so pale !
For want of some foolish words
  Shall the faith of a woman fail ?
Words ! he said them once—
  What need of anything more ?
Does one who has entered a room
  Go back and wait at the door ?

Baby Mary and Kate
  Never can climb his knee ;
Mother's arms are open,
  But " Father's busy, you see " :

Too busy to stop to hear
  A babble of broken talk,
To mend the jumping-jack,
  Or make the new doll walk :

So busy that when death comes
  He pleads for a little delay,
If not to finish his work,
  At the least a word to say—
A word to wife and child,
  A sentence to tell the truth
That he loves them now, at the last,
  With the passionate heart of youth.

The kisses of Death are cold,
  And they turn his lips to stone ;
Out of the warm bright world
  The man goes all alone.

Do angels wait for him there
Over the soundless sea ?
He goes as he came, all helpless,
To a new world's mystery—
Like a child.

LOOKING INTO THE WELL.

Up in the maples the robins sung,
  The winds blew over the locusts high,
And along the path by their boughs o'erhung
  We wandered gaily—Lulu and I—
Wandered along in pleasant talk,
  Pausing our nursery tales to tell,
Till we came to the end of the shaded walk,
  And sat, at last, by the moss-grown well.
She was a child, and so was I,
  It mattered not if we told our love—
Whispered it there, with no one nigh
  Save birds that sang in the trees above.

I looked down into her shy blue eyes,
   She at my face in the shaded well ;
I saw the glow to her fair cheek rise
   Like red in the heart of an ocean shell.

Again in the trees the robins sung—
   The gold had deepened upon her hair—
The locusts over the pathway hung,
   To look at her face so still and fair.
I said no word ; I sat by her side,
   Contented to hold her hand in mine,
Dreaming of love and a fair young bride—
   Visions that truth would have made divine.
The robins' song took a clearer tone,
   The sky was a tenderer, deeper blue ;
Her face in the limpid waters shone,
   I thought her eyes were holy and true.

I walked alone to the shaded well,

　When locusts bloomed in the next year's June;

The shadows along my pathway fell,

　The wild birds sang a sorrowful tune :

She had given her shining hair's young gold,

　Her holy brow, and her eyes of blue,

The form I had scarcely dared to fold,

　To a wealthy suitor who came to woo—

Sold, for jewels and land and name,

　Youth and beauty and love and grace—

Alone I cursed the sin and shame,

　And started to see my own dark face

Mirrored there in the well below,

　With its haggard cheek and its lines of care,

Where I once had seen a girlish brow,

　And shy blue eyes and golden hair.

Years have passed since that summer day

　Went over the hills with its silent tread :

I walk alone where its glory lay—
    I am lonely, and Lulu is dead.
Dust is thick on her shining hair,
    A shroud is folded across her breast,
The winds blow over the locusts where
    She lies at last, alone and at rest.
Youth and beauty, and love and grace,
    Wealth and station, and joy and pain ;
If she dream at all in that lonely place,
    She will know, at length, that her life was vain.

I do not think of her heart's disgrace,
    Looking into the waters there,
For I seem to see once more a face
    With shy blue eyes and golden hair.
Out among men she walks by my side—
    For me she lives whom the world calls dead—
I talk at night to my shadow bride,
    And pillow in dreams her golden head.

They broke her heart—so the gossips tell—
  Who sold her hand for wealth and a name ;
But I see her face in the cool, deep well,
  And its innocent beauty is still the same.

TROTHPLIGHT.

(FOR THE GOLDEN WEDDING OF A HUSBAND THIRTY-SEVEN YEARS BLIND.) ·

I BROUGHT her home, my bonny bride,
    Just fifty years ago ;
Her eyes were bright,
Her step was light,
    Her voice was sweet and low.

In April was our wedding-day—
    The maiden month, you know,
Of tears and smiles,
And wilful wiles,
    And flowers that spring from snow.

My love cast down her dear, dark eyes
        As if she fain would hide
From my fond sight
Her own delight,
        Half shy yet happy bride.

But blushes told the tale instead,
        As plain as words could speak,
In dainty red
That overspread
        My darling's dainty cheek.

For twice six years and more I watched
        Her fairer grow each day—
My babes were blest
Upon her breast,
        And she was pure as they.

And then an angel touched my eyes,
     And turned my day to night,.
That fading charms
Or time's alarms
     Might never vex my sight.

Thus, sitting in the dark, I see
     My darling as of yore—
With blushing face
And winsome grace,
     Unchanged, for evermore.

Full fifty years of young and fair !—
     To her I pledge my vow
Whose spring-time grace
And April face
     Have lasted until now.

FROM DUSK TO DAWN.

It was just at the close of a summer day,
  When the fair young moon in the east was up,
And falling, as falls the peace of God,
  The dew dropped balm in the wild-flower's cup ;

And soft south winds touched the weary brow
  Of a woman who leaned on a cottage-gate,
And lingered to catch the low, sweet call
  Of a late bird singing home to his mate.

From within she heard the household talk,
  As if each to other were true and dear,
And after her, down the lonesome street,
  Followed the sound of mirthful cheer.

They were blest, she **knew**, in their homely peace—
  A sad smile trembled about her mouth—
" I am glad," she said, " that for some poor souls
  There be full wells, though the rest have drouth."

She saw the children about the doors,
  With fond young lips for mothers to kiss,
And from every home, as she passed along,
  She caught some cadence of household bliss.

Till she came, at last, to her own low roof,
  Where she and a ghost dwelt face to face—
The ghost of her days of joy and youth,
  The only guest in that empty place.

They talked together of all the past—
  She and the ghost, in the white moonlight—
Till the pale guest's face like an angel's grew,
  An ancient glory had made it bright.

When the new dawn rose, they both were gone—
    On the bed a shape like the woman's lay—
But she, with the ghost of the gay, glad past,
    To some land of shadows had wandered away ;

A land where she found the lost again —
    Where youth was waiting, and love was sweet,
And all the joys she had buried once
    Sprang up like blossoms about her feet.

JOHN A. ANDREW.

O LARGE of heart, and grand, and calm,
  Who held the helm of state so long,
Our plaining mingles with our praise,
  Our sorrow sanctifies our song.

Clear eyes, kind lips, so silent now,
  Ears deaf to all our worldly din,
Great soul which has not left its peer,
  We would the grave-sod had shut in

Some lesser man, and we, to-day,
  Had thy strong will to urge us on,
Thy brain to plan, thy hands to help,
  Thy cheerful voice to say " Well done !"

But, whatsoe'er we do of good,
　In doing it we honour thee ;
We follow where our leader led—
　Can he look down from heaven and see ?

A WOMAN'S WAITING.

UNDER the apple-tree blossoms, in May,
  Robert and I watched the sun go down ;
Behind us the road stretched back to the east,
  On, through the meadows, to Danbury town.

Silent we sat, for our hearts were full,
  Silently watched the reddening sky,
And saw the clouds across the west
  Like the phantoms of ships sail silently.

Robert had come with a story to tell,
  I knew it before he said a word—
It looked from his eyes, and it shadowed his face—
  He was going to march with the Twenty-third.

We had been neighbours from childhood up—
  Gone to school by the self-same way,
Climbed the same steep woodland paths,
  Knelt in the same old church to pray :

We had wandered together, boy and girl,
  Where wild flowers grew and wild grapes hung ;
Tasted the sweetness of summer days
  When hearts were true and life was young ;

But never a love-word had crossed his lips,
  Never a hint of pledge or vow,
Until, as the sun went down that night,
  His tremulous kisses touched my brow.

" Jenny," he said, " I've a work to do
  For God and my country and the right—
True hearts, strong arms, are needed now,
  I must not linger when others fight.

"Will you give me a pledge to cheer me on—
A hope to look forward to by-and-by?
Will you wait for me, Jenny, till I come back?"
" I will wait," I answered, " until I die."

The May moon rose as we walked that night
Back through the meadows to Danbury town,
And one star rose and shone by her side—
Calmly and sweetly they both looked down.

The scent of blossoms was in the air,
The sky was blue, and the eve was bright,
And Robert said, as he walked by my side,
" Old Danbury town is fair, to-night.

" I shall think of it, Jenny, when far away,
Placid and still 'neath the moon as now—
I shall see it, darling, in many a dream,
And you with the moonlight on your brow."

No matter what else were his parting words—
　They are mine to treasure until I die,
With the clinging kisses and lingering looks,
　The tender pain of that fond good-bye.

I did not weep—I tried to be brave—
　I watched him till he was out of sight—
Then suddenly all the world grew dark,
　And I was blind in the bright May night.

Blind and helpless I slid to the ground
　And lay with the night-dews on my hair,
Till the moon was down, and the dawn was up,
　And the fresh May morn rose clear and fair.

He was taken and I was left—
　Left to wait and to watch and pray—
Till there came a message over the wires,
　Chilling the air of the August day :—

Killed in a skirmish eight or ten—
   Wounded and helpless as many more—
All of them our Connecticut men—
   From the little town of Danbury, four.

But I only saw a single name—
   Of one who was all the world to me :
I promised to wait for him till I died—
   O God, O Heaven, how long will it be?

THE COUNTRY OF "IF."

THERE is not much, indeed, that I can say,
   Since " If " was the sole country of our dreams,
And at its gate One stood to bar our way
   To that glad Land, those silver-shining streams.

I know, dear Heart, how fair that country is—
   Its rivers flow through meadows green and still,
Its skies bend lovingly o'er lovers' bliss,
   No cold winds blow there, and no winters chill.

There would we fain have wandered, thou and I—
   But the strong angel met us at its gate :
He heeded not Love's prayer, or Passion's cry—
   "Oh fools, and mad," he said, "you come too
      late."

FOR CUPID DEAD.

WHEN Love is dead, what more but funeral rites—
   To lay his sweet corse lovingly to rest,
To cover him with rose and eglantine,
   And all fair posies that he loved the best?

What more, but kisses for his close-shut eyes—
   His cold, still lips that never more will speak—
His hair, too bright for dust of death to dim—
   The flush scarce faded from his frozen cheek?

What more, but tears that will not warm his brow,
   Although they burn the eyes from which they
     start?—
No bitter weeping or more bitter words
   Can rouse to one more throb that pulseless heart.

So dead he is, who once was so alive !
  In summer, when the ardent days were long,
He was as warm as June, as gay and glad
  As any bird that swelled its throat with song.

So dead !—yet all things were his ministers—
  All birds and blossoms, and the joyous June ;
Would they had died, and kept sweet Love alive ;
  Since he is gone the world is out of tune.

WE LAY US DOWN TO SLEEP.

WE lay us down to sleep,
   And leave to God the rest ;
Whether to wake and weep,
   Or wake no more be best.

Why vex our souls with care?
   The grave is cool and low ;
Have we found life so fair
   That we should dread to go?

We've kissed love's sweet, red lips,
  And left them sweet and red ;
The rose the wild bee sips
  Blooms on when he is dead.

Some faithful friends we've found,
  But they who love us best,
When we are underground,
  Will laugh on with the rest.

No task have we begun
  But other hands can take ;
No work beneath the sun
  For which we need to wake.

Then hold us fast, sweet Death,
  If so, it seemeth best
To Him who gave us breath
  That we should go to rest.

We lay us down to sleep,
   Our weary eyes we close ;
Whether to wake and weep,
   Or wake no more, He knows.

THE END.

CHARLES DICKENS AND EVANS, CRYSTAL PALACE PRESS

www.ingramcontent.com/pod-product-compliance
Lightning Source LLC
Chambersburg PA
CBHW030905050726
47500CB00009B/1098